Day Care is for Everyone

Book 4 of the

Mr. Nibbles' Bites of Life

Series

By Mr. Nibbles and

Leslie Goodale Adebonojo

Spring Knoll Press

2019

This book is a work of fiction. The character in this story, Mr. Nibbles, does not represent any other dog. Any resemblance to any other dog living or dead is entirely coincidental.

Mr. Nibbles Bites' of Life Series

Let Sleeping Dogs Lie Book 1

Chasing the Moon Book 2

Vegetables are for Eating Book 3

Published in the United States

Spring Knoll Press

ISBN 9780997874679

For Geoff

My inspiration.

Love Mom

A big thank you to everyone at Camp Ruff N More for taking care of Mr. Nibbles when he comes to day care

and especially to Julie for the picture of Mr. Nibbles and Jazzie.

Discussions and observations that you may want to have with your child.

This book is designed to encourage children to create their own story to go along with the pictures.

To find out more about shadows go to:

https://www.dkfindout.com/us/science/light/shadows/

To find out more about why it is good to drink water go to:

https://www.healthykids.nsw.gov.au/kids-teens/choose-water-as-a-drink-kids

Mr. Nibbles came from a local animal shelter to live with us. He loves to run outside, sleep, play ball, chase the Moon and go to day care camp to play with his friends.

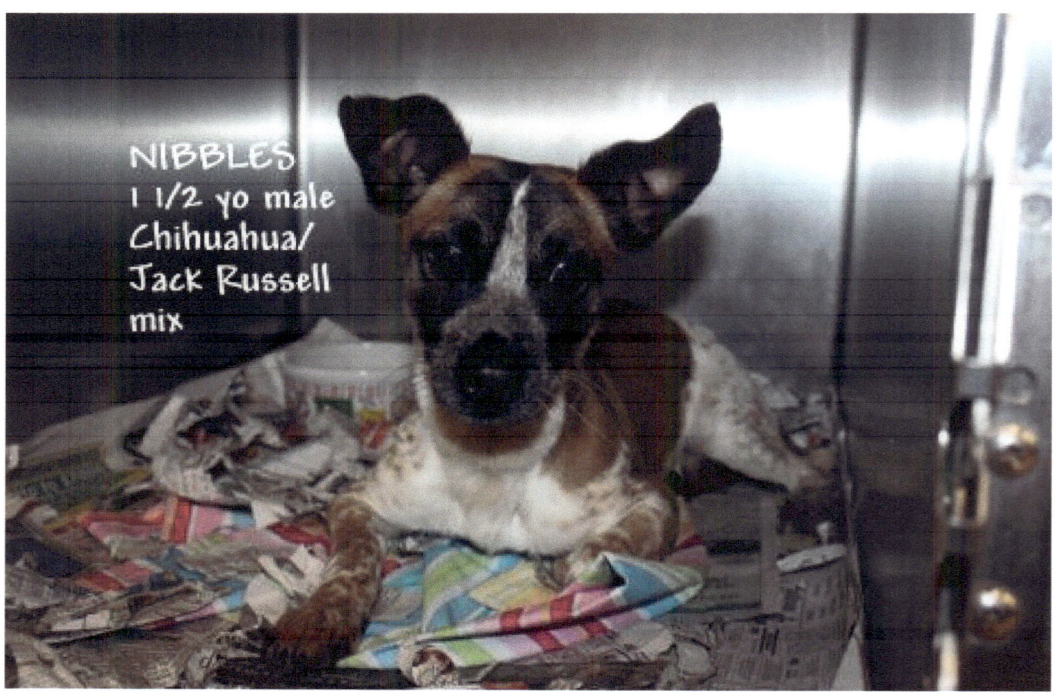

NIBBLES
1 1/2 yo male
Chihuahua/
Jack Russell
mix

Mr. Nibbles is waiting to go to day care camp. He loves to play with his friends when he gets there.

Mr. Nibbles travels in his crate in the car to and from day care. What else is in the car for Mr. Nibbles?

Waiting to go inside to the playroom.

At the check-in desk.

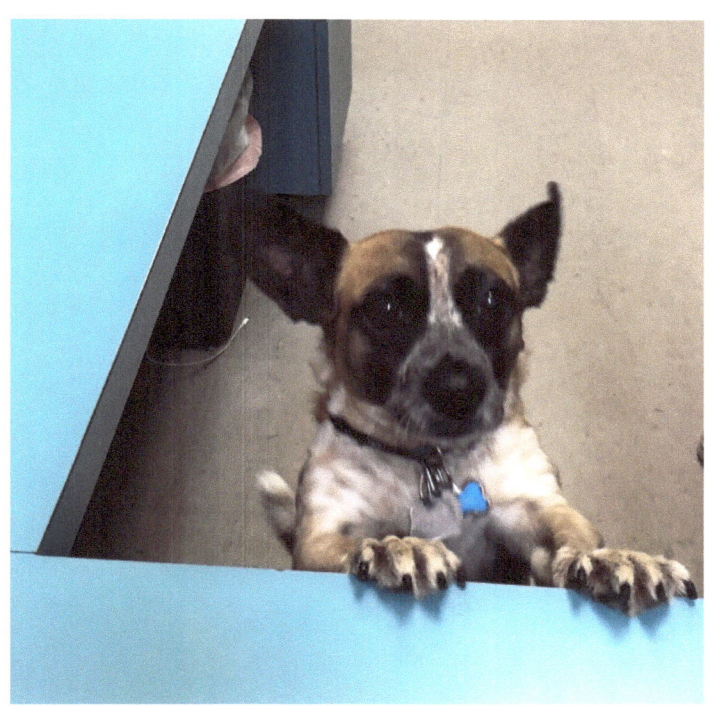

Mr. Nibbles has human friends at day care camp.

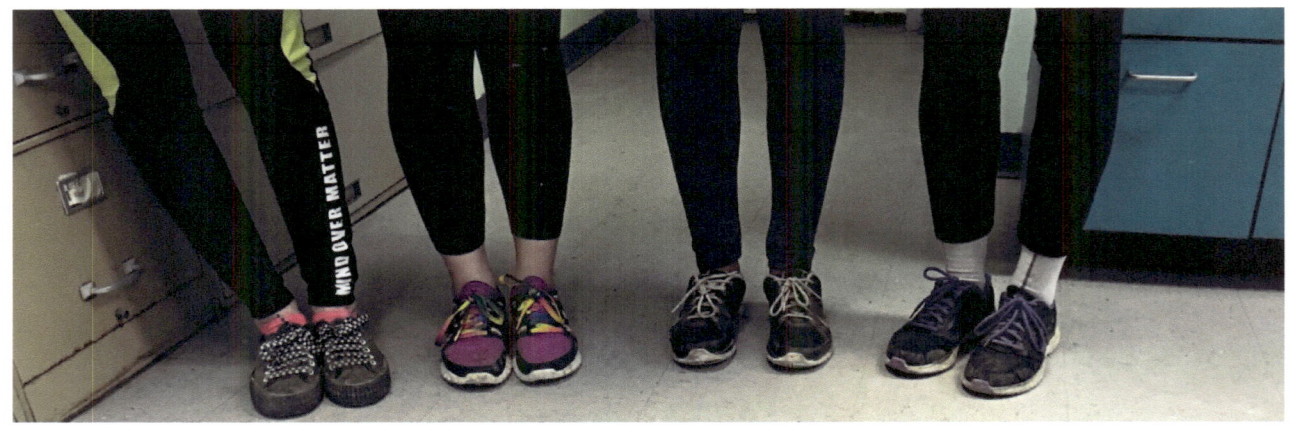

Can you count the number of human friends in the picture? How many are there?

Mr. Nibbles loves to play at day care camp – he does not take a nap – he runs around all day.

Where is Mr. Nibbles? How many friends does Mr. Nibbles have at day care?

Is Mr. Nibbles getting ready to do something?

What is Mr. Nibbles getting ready to do?
Who is watching Mr. Nibbles?

Here I go. I can make it to the top of the door. Zoe and Maynard think Mr. Nibbles can make it to the top. Do you think he can?

What did Mr. Nibbles do? Where did he go?

Sometimes Mr. Nibbles likes to sit outside with his friend Jazzie.

When the weather is nice, they have a big playground to run in. Do some of the play structures look like the ones you have at your playground?

Bye, Bye friends.
Time for me to go home.

Mr. Nibbles is thirsty after he plays at day care camp.

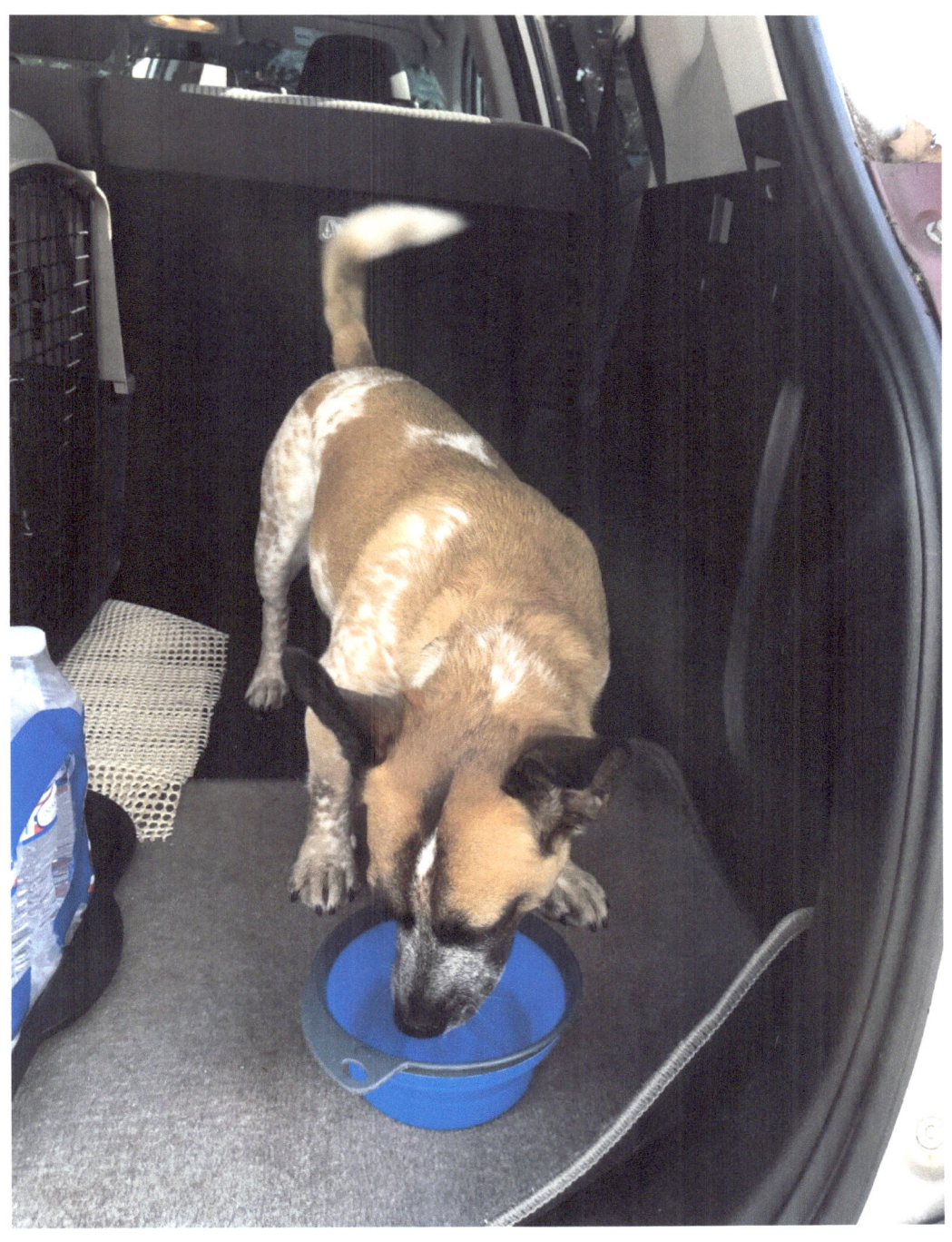

I just want to take a nap.

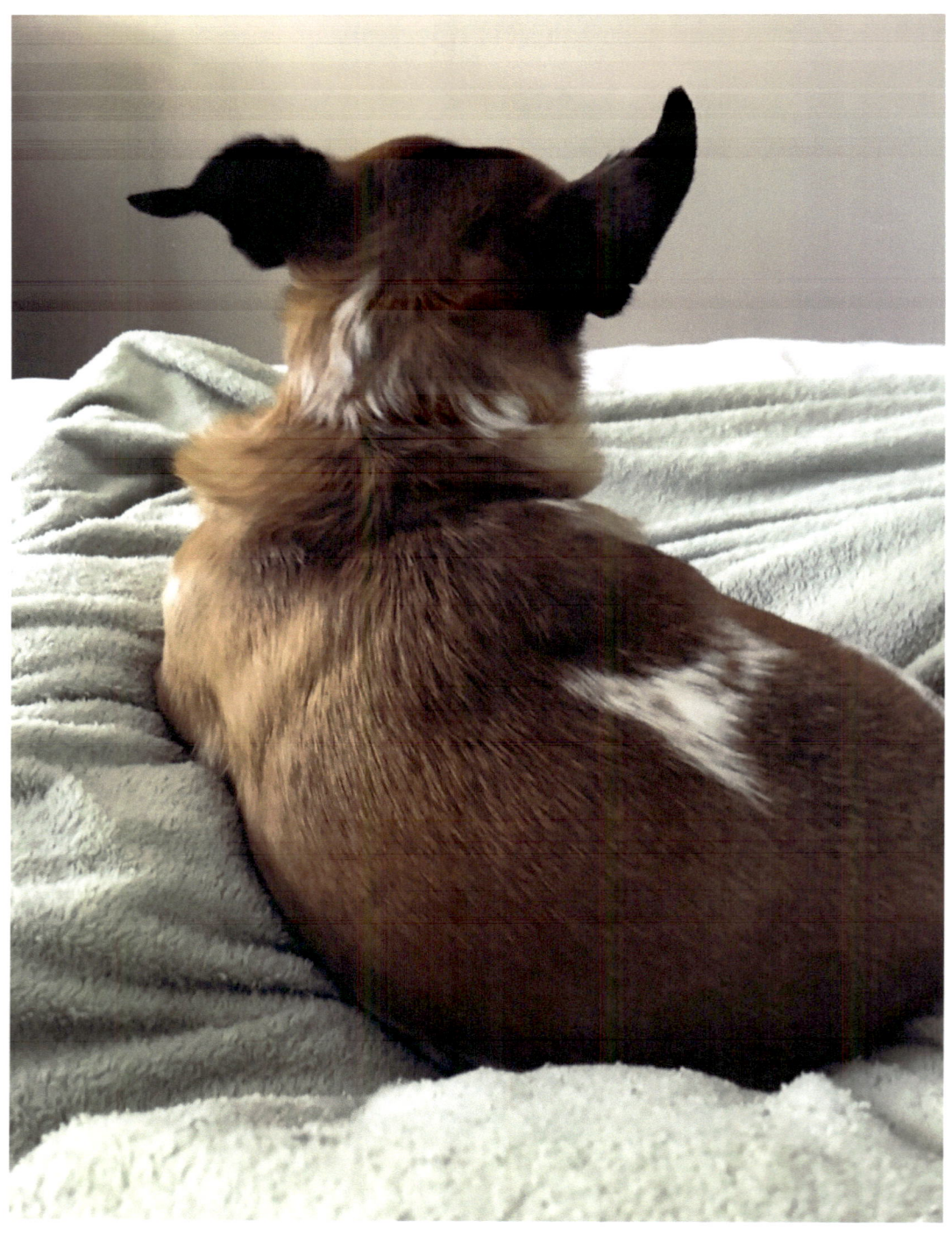

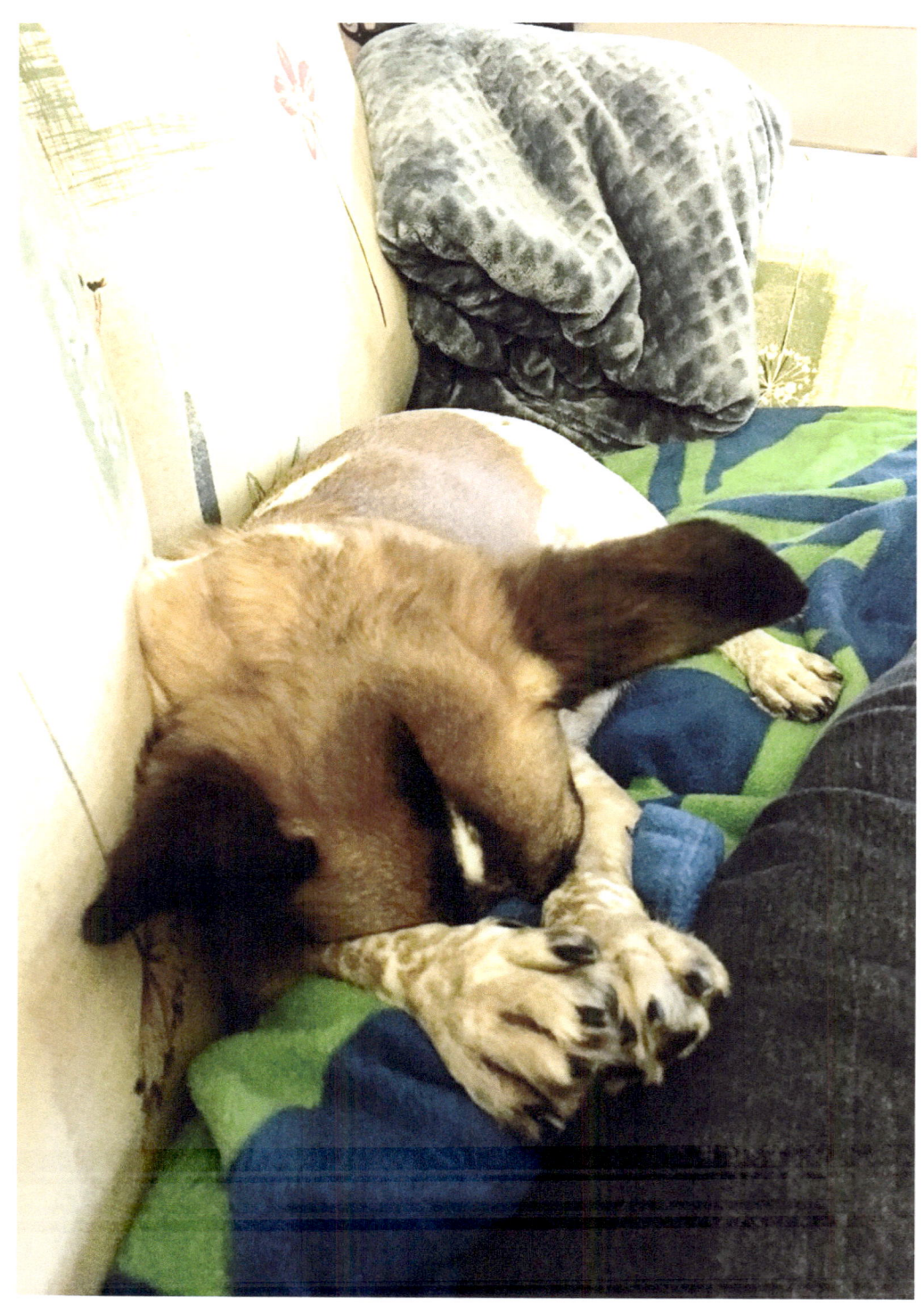

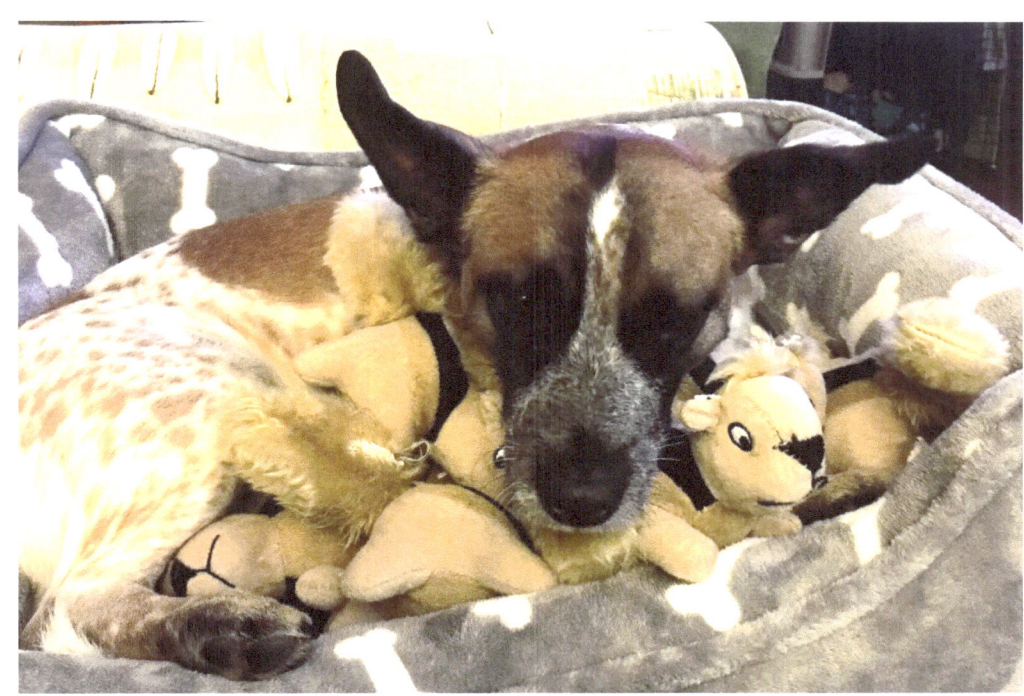

Napping
with
friends
at home.

Awake but still tired.

Outside to run and play.

What is running beside Mr. Nibbles?
Is it his shadow?

Mr. Nibbles likes his treats.

Home again to take another nap.
Do you see Mr. Nibbles?

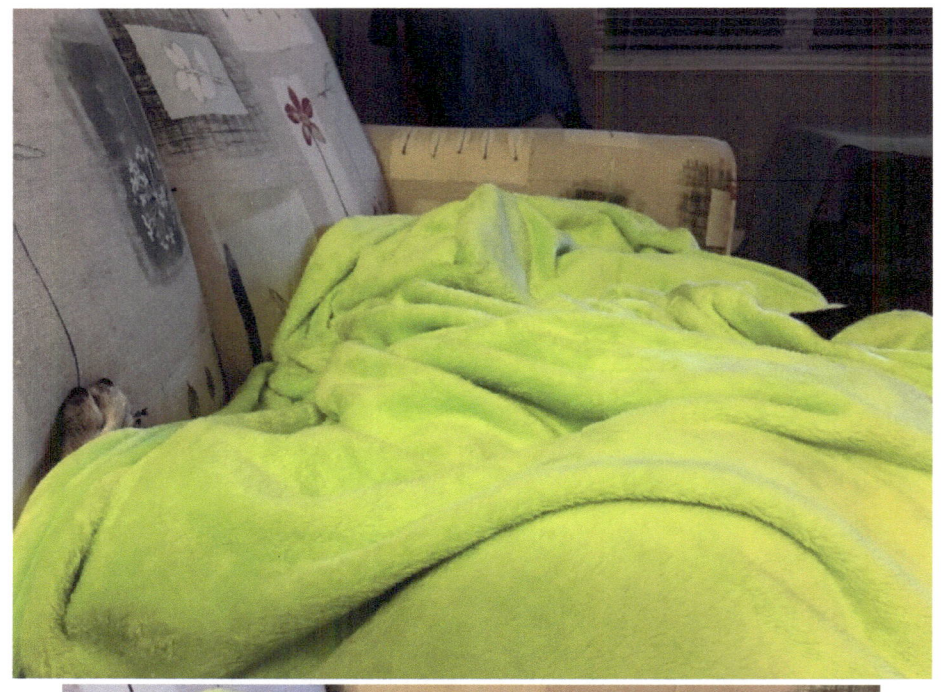

When Mr. Nibbles gets up from his nap he likes to eat a snack. What is Mr. Nibbles looking at in the refrigerator?

Carrots of course.